Pump the Bear ™

By Gisella Olivo Whittington

illustrations by Joseph Crisalli

Pump the Bear

ISBN: 0-9706038-0-0
Printed in Korea

Published by Brown Books • 16200 North Dallas Parkway, Suite 225, Dallas, Texas 75248 • www.brownbooks.com

Once upon a time, there was a family called the Whittington Bears. There was a Papa Bear, a Mama Bear, and two sister bears named Brit and Lexi. They were a very happy family, but they had just one wish . . . a baby brother bear.

One sunny day, their wish came true.

They were blessed with a baby brother cub.

They were all very happy. But soon after, the

doctor came with bad news. "Your baby cub

is sick and was born with a broken heart.

We know this because his face is a bit blue,"

the doctor said.

Then, the Whittington Bears were sad.

They felt as though their hearts had been

broken too!

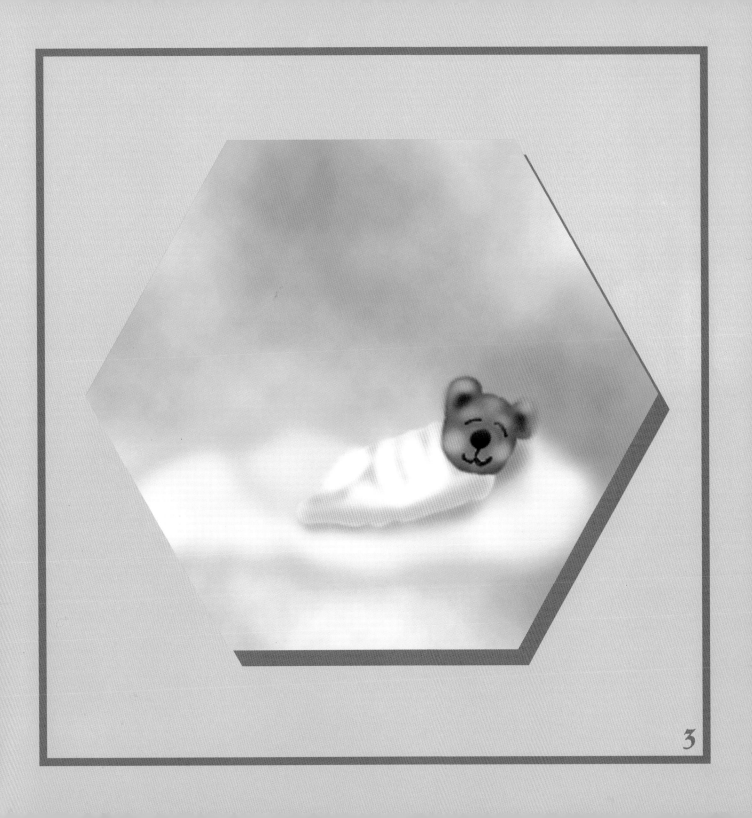

3

The Whittingtons named the baby cub, Pump. Pump and his family lived in a small forest. He needed help quickly, so Pump was flown in a fast airplane to a big city hospital. In this hospital, the doctors would fix Pump's broken heart.

Many family and friends from Pump's home in the forest joined together to help. People from all over the world prayed for a miracle to save Pump. They formed a circle and prayed that his little broken heart would be fixed.

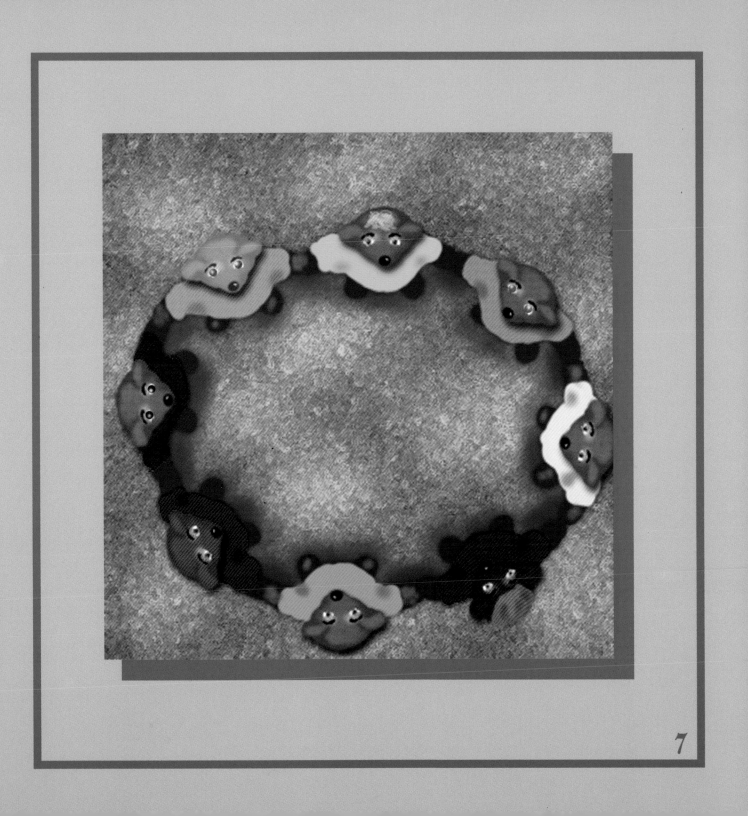

7

After many hours of surgery, the doctors and nurses mended Pump's broken heart. Everyone was hopeful. But, several hours later, Pump began to feel like his heart was breaking again.

Suddenly, a light filled the room and Pump's guardian angel appeared. She was so beautiful and her wings were soft and fluffy. The angel wrapped her wings around little Pump. Her hug comforted him by filling his heart with love, strength and courage.

The room became very peaceful. Pump's heart felt warm and fuzzy. He felt a special power in him . . . like a glowing light. He slowly began to feel strong inside. Pump fought hard to be well.

9

As Pump grew older, his heart got stronger. Pump grew up to be a healthy and happy bear. He is just like any normal little bear who sometimes gets himself into trouble. But, Mama still calls Pump her special "Angel Bear."

Every night before bedtime, Mama Bear and Pump spend time reading books and talking about life. He was a very curious bear and always had a lot of questions.

"Mama, am I special?" he asked.

"Yes, my precious son," she answered.

"Why?" he asked.

"Everybody on this earth is special because everyone is unique. We all have a special gift and it's up to us to find out what it is," she said.

"What's my special gift?" Pump asked.

"My beloved, to find your gift you need to do three things. One, you need to be very quiet. Two, you need to close your eyes. Three, you need to listen to your heart. When you connect your mind with your heart, you will find the answer," Mama Bear explained.

"Okay, it's bedtime and you need a good night's rest," Mama said as Pump snuggled into his pillow.

As she went to shut off the light, Pump said, "Mama, I'm afraid of the dark."

Mama put on some soft music to help relax him and reached over to give Pump a good night kiss and hug. "Think about all the happy things you love to do. I love you," she said softly.

"I love you too, Mama!" he responded.

With happy tears in her eyes, Mama Bear closed the door. Pump was very quiet, closed his eyes and listened to his heart.

Pump started thinking about all the things he loved to do. "I love to play sports, I love to read, I love music, I love eating oats, I love school, I love spending time with my family, I love hugs, I love . . . Zzzzzz . . ."

Soon, loving thoughts filled his mind and he fell fast asleep. In his peaceful dream something amazing happened! Pump felt so much love that a glow suddenly filled his heart. He felt that warm and fuzzy feeling and the angel's wings comforting him. He soon found the answer!

The next day Pump woke up yelling, "Mama, Papa, Brit, Lexi . . . I know what my special gift is!" His heart was beating faster and faster. He was so excited he tripped over his toys, landed on his skateboard and ran into a big bowl of fruit.

"It's my heart! I have a special heart! First it was broken, but now it is fixed. I have a whole big heart so now I can share it with others who need some love. Also, when I am feeling sad, I have the power inside my heart to make myself feel better."

"That's right, son," said Papa Bear. "Our hearts are very important. We only have one heart so we have to take good care of it. We should try to eat healthy, exercise and never smoke!"

All the Whittington Bears have healthy hearts. They go to the doctor every year for check-ups to make sure their hearts are pumping well. They also love to do family activities like taking walks through the forest. Their happy hearts are smiling inside and are filled with love. Together, they live happily and healthily ever after.

The Happy Ending

Pump Ponders

Questions from a curious,
lovable and huggable bear...

22

What is heart disease?

The heart is a muscle that pumps blood to the head and the body. The blood travels through tubes in your body called veins and arteries. Heart disease is when the heart has a problem or condition that will not allow it to work in a normal way. We are so fortunate that we are learning more and more about the heart and heart disease each year through research. Millions of people are being saved each year. It's important to know the risk factors so we can protect our heart for a lifetime.

Why do I need yearly doctor check-ups?

You are a special person who is very loved and your family and friends want you to be healthy. We must get a check-up even when we are feeling well. Sometimes we may look okay on the outside and feel good on the inside, but only the doctor can tell if you are really healthy. You can sometimes prevent some illnesses if a problem is noticed early enough.

What is prevention?

Prevention is when you stop something from happening. You can prevent some diseases by making some positive changes in your life, like eating healthy, exercising and never smoking.

Why is smoking bad for me?

Smoking is a choice some people make, but it is a bad choice for your health. Smoking is a major risk factor for heart disease. There is a chemical called Nicotine in cigarettes. When you smoke, this chemical goes into your body and makes your heart beat faster. When your heart beats faster, the blood travels through your veins and arteries faster. Nicotine makes your arteries become narrow, so the heart has to work really hard to pump the blood through. This hurts your heart and your entire body.

Why should I stay active?

Exercise is good for your heart, lungs, bones and muscles. It gives you lots of energy and makes you strong. Exercise also can help you relax and sleep better. You should do fun and easy activities like walking in the park. You should also do more difficult activities like playing sports, jumping rope, swimming or running.

What are some healthy foods for me?

You should choose a variety of foods and make sure you don't over eat. Some foods have more nutrients than others do. Some good choices of foods to eat would be cereal, oatmeal, apples, carrots, fish, beans, soy, juice and fat free milk. Also, drink lots of water!

Why is music good for me?

Music has been used as a way of calming the heart, mind, body and soul for thousands of years. Studies have proven that soft music can make you healthier. The most effective music for health purposes is that which is played at 60 beats per minute. This is the speed of a sleeping person's heartbeat or a person in deep meditation.

Do my feelings inside affect my heart?

Yes. If you are feeling sad, remember that you are special and that somebody cares about you. You should always talk to somebody about your feelings and never keep them inside. There is a good reason you are having these feelings. Talk to your parents, a doctor or even a friend. They will listen to you and help you feel better.

How can I learn more about my health?

Read, read and read! Read as much as you can about this subject. Education is prevention. Knowledge, when combined with action, always equals power! Encourage the whole family to get involved. Parents should set a good example. It's best to learn healthy habits when the children are young. These habits can make a big difference in the future of our health.

For more information about living a heart-healthy lifestyle, additional copies of this book, the Pump the Bear™ stuffed animal, the CD (at 60 beats per minute) or Wyatt's Heart Foundation, go to:

www.pumpuplife.com
www.wyattsheart.org
www.americanheart.org

The information contained in this book is no substitute for medical advice or treatment. The American Heart Association recommends consultation with a doctor or health care professional.